Lottie and Dottie Sow Carrots

There are lots of Early Reader
stories you might enjoy.

Look at the back of the book
or, for a complete list, visit
www.orionbooks.co.uk

Lottie and Dottie Sow Carrots

By Claire Burgess

Illustrated by
Marijke van Veldhoven

Orion
Children's Books

First published in Great Britain in 2014
by Orion Children's Books
a division of the Orion Publishing Group Ltd
Orion House
5 Upper Saint Martin's Lane
London WC2H 9EA
An Hachette UK company

1 3 5 7 9 10 8 6 4 2

Text © Claire Burgess 2014
Illustrations © Marijke van Veldhoven 2014

The moral right of Claire Burgess and Marijke van Veldhoven to be
identified as author and illustrator of this work has been asserted.

The Orion Publishing Group's policy is to use papers that are natural,
renewable and recyclable products and made from wood grown in
sustainable forests. The logging and manufacturing processes are expected
to conform to the environmental regulations of the country of origin.

ISBN 978 1 4440 1128 9

A catalogue record for this book is available from the British Library.

Printed and bound in China

www.orionbooks.co.uk

*For Mark, Emily and George,
who love to eat whatever size,
shape or colour carrots
I decide to grow.*

This is Lottie and this is her little sister Dottie.

They live in a village called Greenville. Lottie and Dottie love growing things, but their garden is very small, so they grow most of their plants in pots.

"Yippee! At last it's spring,"
said Dottie. She was so excited.
"I've been waiting for it all
winter and now it's here. Can
we start sowing seeds today?"

"Yes," said Lottie.

As they crunched their cornflakes
Dottie wondered what to sow.

A lettuce?

A tomato?

Or a
sunflower?

After breakfast they skipped off to Mr McWelly's Garden Centre. "Wow!" said Dottie. "This place is huge, you could fit the whole world in here."

"This is where they sell seeds,"
said Lottie. "Let's go and see if
we can find them."

As they went in they saw the owner, Mr McWelly.
"Hello," he said. "What brings you here today?"
"We've come to buy some seeds," said Dottie.
"They're over there," said Mr McWelly.

Lottie held Dottie's hand. They passed all sorts of useful things you need in the garden.

"Are we nearly there?" asked
Dottie. "I've only got little legs."

Suddenly Dottie stopped. She had
seen Mr Thompson.
He lived near Lottie and Dottie.

He was always digging holes in
his garden. Dottie wondered what
they were for. He looked grumpy.

Dottie was scared. Her eyes opened wide, and she ran to Lottie.

Lottie and Dottie found the seeds.
There were hundreds of packets
all lined up.
"Oh, wow! There are so many,"
said Dottie.

"Shall I choose today?" said
Lottie.
"Can I?" asked Dottie.
"Of course you can," Lottie said
smiling.
Dottie gave her a hug.

Dottie stared at the packets of seeds in front of her. Then she sat down on the floor.

"Would you like some help?"
asked Lottie.
"No, thank you," said Dottie.
Lottie sat next to her.

Then Lottie asked, "What's your
favourite colour?"
"I don't know," said Dottie.

She looked down at her boots and
wiggled her feet. She smiled.
"Orange," she said.

"We can't grow an orange.
Is there anything else that is
orange?" asked Lottie.
"Carrots are orange," said Dottie.
"Yes they are. Well done," said
Lottie.

She found the packets of carrot seeds, but there were lots to choose from.

"Look," said Lottie. "They've got purple carrots, orange carrots, rainbow carrots, round carrots and black carrots. Which one shall we choose?"

Dottie thought. "Orange carrots," she said.

"Will we have them for tea?"
asked Dottie.
"They won't grow **that** fast,"
said Lottie.

As they came to the till, Dottie
stopped again.
Mr Thompson was walking
towards them taking giant steps.
The ground shook as he got
closer. He crouched down.
Dottie squeaked.

"Hello," he said gently. "What have you got there?"
"Carrot seeds," said Lottie.

"May I see?" he said.
Dottie showed him, but she still
felt scared.
"I'll tell you a secret," said
Mr Thompson.

"What did he say?" asked Lottie.
"Oh, nothing," said Dottie.

They waved goodbye to
Mr McWelly.
"See you again soon,"
he called.

"First we need a large pot,"
said Lottie.
"Like this?" said Dottie.

"No, that's too small," Lottie said. "We need something much bigger."

"Is this one big enough?" Dottie asked.

"I can't see anything," came
Dottie's muffled voice.

"Silly sausage," said Lottie.
Lottie took the pot off Dottie's
head.

"I know a secret," Dottie
whispered.

"What?" asked Lottie.
"Mr Thompson told me,"
she said.
"Will it help us grow our
carrots?" Lottie asked.
Dottie nodded.
"Then you can tell me,"
said Lottie.

"Mr Thompson said not to have many stones in the soil," said Dottie. "Why?" asked Lottie. "So the carrots can grow really long," said Dottie.

"Then we'll just put a few stones
at the bottom, and fill the rest
of the pot with compost."
"What's compost?" asked Dottie.
"It's like soil. It helps the plants
grow," said Lottie.

"If I stand in compost will I grow?" said Dottie.

"No," said Lottie. "It only works for plants."

They filled the pot almost to the
top with compost.

Then they patted
it down.

Then they gave
the compost
some water.

"Why are we watering the compost?" asked Dottie.
"So the seeds start to grow straight away," said Lottie.
"Will I see them growing?" Dottie asked.
"No, it'll take a little while," said Lottie.

Lottie shook a few seeds into
Dottie's hand.

Then Dottie sprinkled them on
the compost.

"Will we get big, fat carrots?"
asked Dottie.
"If we look after them we should,"
said Lottie. "Now let's cover them
with a bit more compost."
Dottie wrote a label.

"What now?" asked Dottie.
"We wait for them to grow,"
said Lottie.
"How long will that take?"
asked Dottie.
"A little while," said Lottie
again. "But you must check them
every day."

"I'll wear my orange ribbon every day to help them grow," said Dottie.

So every morning Dottie looked
at them.
A week went by.
"Nothing's happening," she said.
"They're not growing."

Then one morning…
"Look, Lottie!" Dottie said.
She could see some tiny green
shoots.
"Aren't they lovely," said Lottie.

Soon more carrots grew, and when
the soil got dry, they watered it.

When summer ended, Lottie said,
"Shall we see if the carrots are
ready?"
"Oh, yes," said Dottie.

"Hold the leaves, give them a wiggle and pull," Lottie said. Dottie took a deep breath and wiggled the carrots. Out they came!

Pop!!

"Look at this one!" yelled Dottie.
"I made a carrot."
"Grew a carrot," said Lottie.
"Let's pull some more, we can
have one each now and we'll
have the rest for tea."

"Let's show Mr Thompson,"
said Dottie.
"Well done," said Mr Thompson.
"You're so clever."
"Thank you," said Dottie.

Just before tea-time Lottie was
looking for Dottie.
"Where are you, Dottie?" she
called.
There was no reply. Lottie went
into the garden.
"Here you are," she said.

"Rabbits like carrots too," said
Dottie.
"Yes they do. Come inside.
Time for tea!" said Lottie.

As they ate tea Lottie and Dottie hardly said a word. They both agreed that carrots taste much better if you grow them yourself.

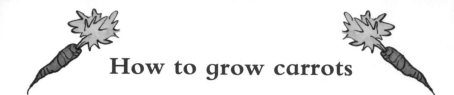

How to grow carrots

Sow your carrot seeds from
March to June.

Two weeks later you will see
green shoots.

Make sure you water them when the soil is dry.

Pull your carrots from July to October when the top of the carrot is about 2cm wide like this.

What are you going to read next?

Have more adventures with Horrid Henry,

and travel the world with Miranda the Explorer.

Play clever tricks with Twit,

spend Mondays at Monster School,

and even brave The Dragon's Dentist . . .

Learn how love is just like a Woolly Hat,

dance under The Little Nut Tree, take home Monstar, the best pet ever, and have an extra-special Mr Monkey birthday party!

Enjoy all the Early Readers.